The Blue China Pitcher

written and illustrated by

Elizabeth C. Meyer

Abingdon Press

Nashville and New York

The Blue China Pitcher

Copyright © 1974 by Abingdon Press

Library of Congress Cataloging in Publication Data

Meyer, Elizabeth, 1958-   The blue china pitcher.

SUMMARY: The pitcher of milk Sarah has placed in the
stream to cool disappears. What will she say when the guests
arrive for tea? I. Title.
      PZ7.M5687B1   [E]   73-15935
            ISBN 0-687-03625-9

To

Mommy and Daddy

and Katherine

One sunny summer morning Sarah decided to have a tea party. She sat down at her large oaken desk and made two pale yellow invitations to send to Oswald Rabbit and Bernard the Woodmouse, two of her best friends in Sourberry Wood.

She gave the invitations to a passing chickadee to be delivered at once.

The chickadee returned later and landed on a dandelion stem. He told Sarah that both of her friends would like very much to come to her tea party.

Oswald, who had been eating his breakfast of raspberries and cream, had been so excited about the party that his little powder puff tail had begun to twitch!

On the day of the party, Sarah was very busy. She baked little cakes and topped them with pink frosting.

She hung the kettle over the fire for tea, and she got out her very best china pitcher for the milk. It was a beautiful pitcher, with little blue flowers all around its sides.

Before the party, Sarah filled the pitcher with milk and set it on a flat rock in Pussywillow Creek where the cool water splashed around it and rushed by it, making the milk cold and pleasing to drink.

Then she went back to her house and changed into a sunny yellow gown she had made herself.

When it was time to fetch the milk, Sarah set out once more for Pussywillow Creek.

There little golden fish swam to and fro in the water, flashing in the sunlight, and singing:

> Gold from the pirates,
> Gold from the king,
> But have you ever met
> A bar of gold that sings?

Sarah looked up and down the creek, but her lovely blue china pitcher was nowhere to be seen! She sat down on a tuft of marsh grass and began to cry.

Nearby, on the branch of a dogwood tree, a little black-capped chickadee chirped to cheer her. Sarah dried her face with a handkerchief and started back to her house. It was almost time for the party.

At four o'clock Oswald and a very furry wood-mouse came down the lane, wearing their best coats. Bernard carried a bunch of violets in his paw, and Oswald carefully brought a lovely blue china pitcher with milk in it!

When Sarah saw her pitcher, she was quite surprised. Oswald explained proudly that he had found it in Pussywillow Creek and that he could think of no better person to give it to than Sarah, "And isn't it beautiful, too," he said.

Sarah hugged both of her friends, and put the violets in a glass vase on the table.

Then they all sat down and had tea together with cold, fresh milk from the little blue pitcher.

Oswald would be unhappy if he knew the blue pitcher had always been Sarah's. Of course, Sarah never told him what he had done.